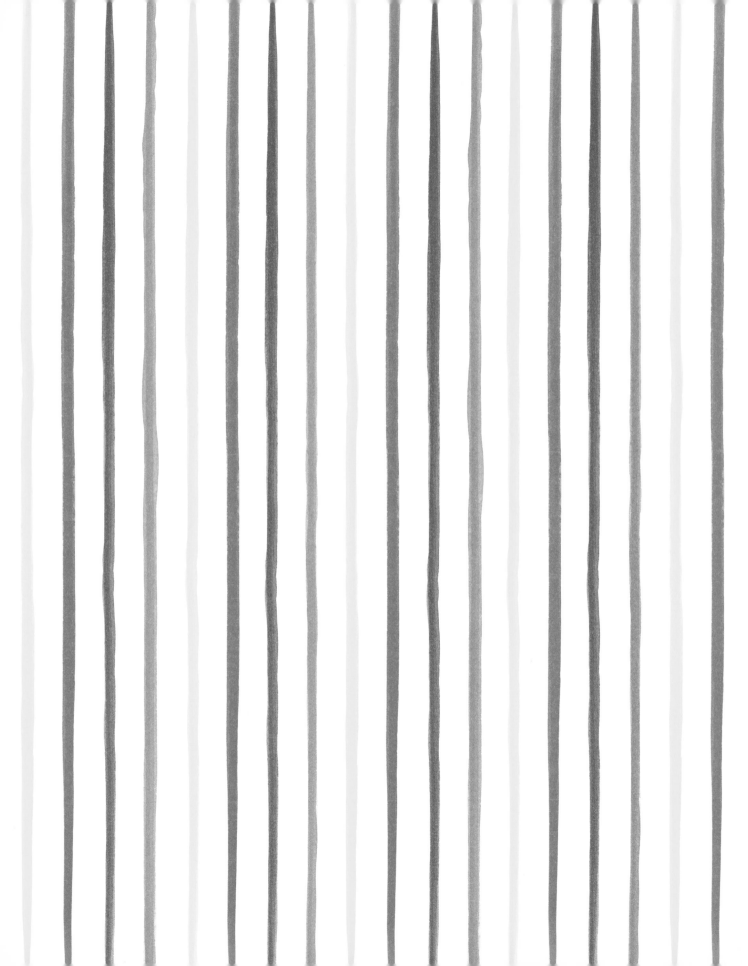

George is a good little monkey,
and always very curious.
George is curious about **you!**

Fill in this book to help George
learn about his new friend—

_____!

(your name)

**Illustrations by
Greg Paprocki and Anna Grossnickle Hines
Written by Monica Perez
Additional concept development by Madeleine Budnick
Designed by Madeleine Budnick**

For information about permission to reproduce
selections from this book, write to Permissions,
Houghton Mifflin Company, 215 Park Avenue South,
New York, New York 10003.

www.houghtonmifflinbooks.com

The text of this book is set in New Century
Schoolbook and Majer Irregular.
The illustrations are watercolor, pencil, and charcoal.
ISBN-13: 978-0-618-73762-8
Printed in Singapore

Curious George and Me!

by

_____

(that's me!)

Houghton Mifflin Company

Boston 2007

Curious About
Me!

Hi!

My name is

_____ (first)

_____ (middle)

_____ (last).

I am a ☐ **girl** ☐ **boy** ☐ **monkey.**

Here is a picture of my family (draw or paste picture):

And here is my **family tree:**

me!

I have __ brother(s) and __ sister(s).

Their names are _____ .

I am a ☐ first ☐ middle ☐ youngest ☐ only child.

**Circle the pets you already have in RED,
and the ones you would like to have in BLUE.**

big dog

little dog

cat

lizard

penguin

My pets' names are

_____

_____

goldfish

rabbit

turtle

giraffe

ants

This is today's date: _____ _____ , _____ .

                                                  (month)   (day)   (year)

I am

1 2 3 4 5   6 7 8 9 10

                                                              (circle)

years old!

MY BIRTH CERTIFICATE

_____ was born

on _____ (month) _____ (day),

_____ (year), at _____ a.m./p.m.

She/He weighed _____ pounds _____ ounces

and was _____ inches long.

I'm growing!

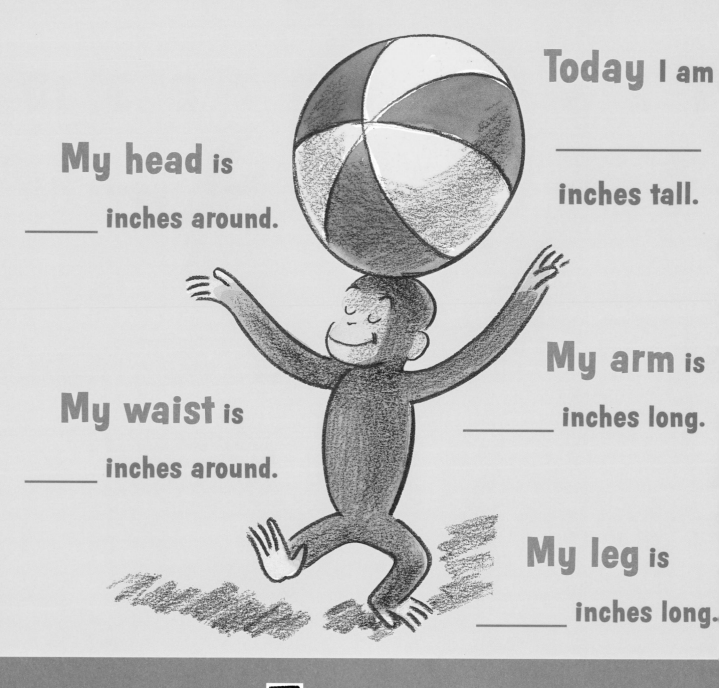

Today I am

_____

inches tall.

My head is

_____ inches around.

My arm is

_____ inches long.

My waist is

_____ inches around.

My leg is

_____ inches long.

I ☐ can
 ☐ cannot
do this trick.

Here is an outline of MY HAND:

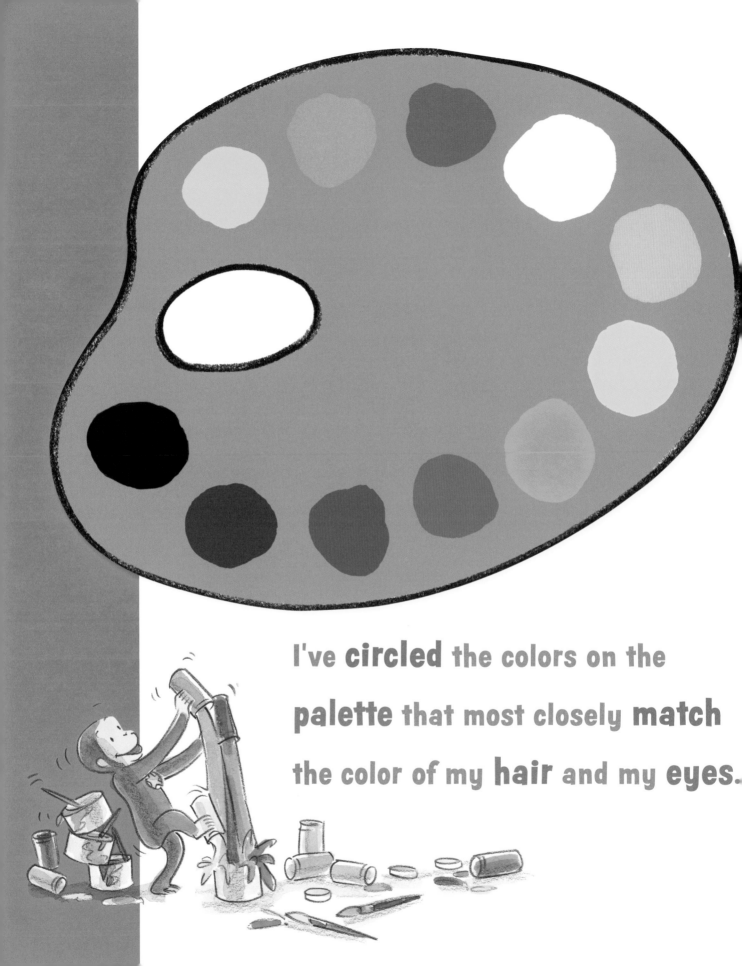

I've **circled** the colors on the **palette** that most closely **match** the color of my **hair** and my **eyes**.

I have ____ teeth
and ____ missing teeth!

This is what I look like when I SMILE (draw):

This is what I like to wear **every** day:

What I like to wear
when I **dress up:**

Curious About
My World!

Curious George left his home in the jungle. He has lived in the city and in the country. My home is most like this one (circle):

hut

birdhouse

apartment

tree house

pueblo

houseboat

igloo

house

cabin

castle

trailer

skyscraper

You can send me a letter at this address:

....

....

....

I ☐ have ☐ have not   always lived here.

ALABAMA

ALASKA

ARIZONA

ARKANSAS

CALIFORNIA

COLORADO

CONNECTICUT

DELAWARE

FLORIDA

GEORGIA

HAWAII

IDAHO

ILLINOIS

INDIANA

IOWA

KANSAS

KENTUCKY

LOUISIANA

MAINE

MARYLAND

MASSACHUSETTS

MICHIGAN

I was born in

_____ (city),

_____ (state).

I found my **HOME STATE** on this map of the United States and have marked it with a .

MINNESOTA

MISSISSIPPI

MISSOURI

MONTANA

NEBRASKA

NEVADA

NEW HAMPSHIRE

NEW JERSEY

NEW MEXICO

NEW YORK

NORTH CAROLINA

NORTH DAKOTA

OHIO

OKLAHOMA

OREGON

PENNSYLVANIA

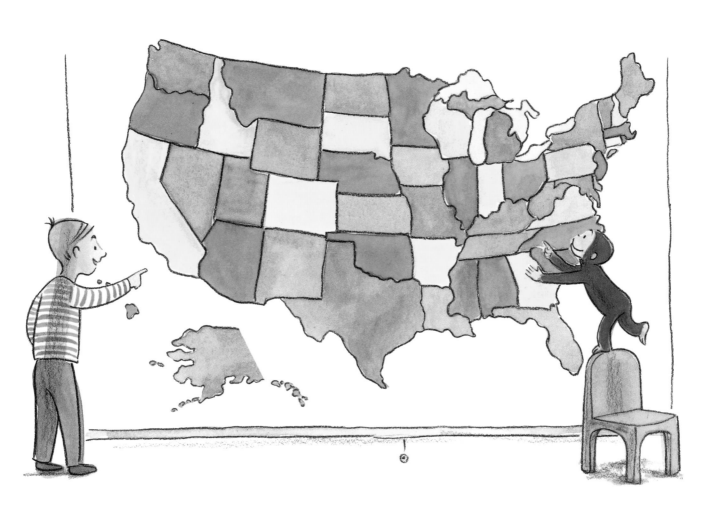

RHODE ISLAND

SOUTH CAROLINA

SOUTH DAKOTA

TENNESSEE

TEXAS

UTAH

VERMONT

VIRGINIA

WASHINGTON

WEST VIRGINIA

WISCONSIN

WYOMING

DISTRICT
OF COLUMBIA

I've circled the STATES I'VE VISITED.

I am ☐ a little ☐ very curious
about other places to live.
If I had the chance to travel ANYWHERE,
I would travel by (circle)...

car

scooter

motorcycle

hot air
balloon

plane

unicycle

rocket

boat

train

submarine

bike

horse

and visit places like (circle)...

the city

the Farm

the DESERT

THE SNOW SLOPE

the beach

THE MOUNTAINS

I can **explore** at home, too!

The **best** secret hiding place in my home is

_____

_____

_____.

I've **collected** some **interesting facts** while exploring my **home**. My home has...

____ **rooms,**   ____ **doors,**

____ **closets,**   ____ **outlets,**

____ **lights,** and ____ **windows!**

☐ I have my own room.

☐ I share a room with

_____ .

Here is a picture of how I've DECORATED my room:

Curious George has a best friend —the man with the yellow hat. They have many adventures.

My friends' names are

_____

_____

_____

_____

_____

My first friend to sleep over was

____ !

We like to do these fun things together:

- ☐ ride bikes
- ☐ sit next to each other in school
- ☐ eat ice cream
- ☐ have sleepovers
- ☐ play sports
- ☐ make things

- ☐ draw pictures and paint
- ☐ solve puzzles
- ☐ go to the movies
- ☐ play games
- ☐ wrestle
- ☐ bake
- ☐ play in the park

The best adventure

my friends and I had was when we

_____

_____

_____

_____ .

Here we are!

(draw or paste photo)

Curious About
What I Like!

These are som

color _____

song _____

place to visit _____

animal _____

toy _____

game _____

# of my favorite things:

movie _____

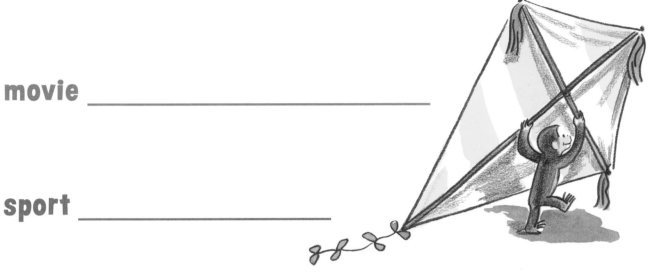

sport _____

ice cream flavor _____

TV show _____

season _____

holiday _____

Curious George LOVES bananas.

☐ I do, too!

☐ They're not for me, thanks!

Curious George also likes...

(I've circled **MY** favorites.)

Foods I **LOVE**:

Some foods that I would be curious to try:

On my **birthday** we eat...

cake

candy

pizza

cupcakes

potato chips

cookies

sandwiches

pie

I invite ☐ friends

☐ family

☐ neighbors

to my BIRTHDAY PARTIES!

We play music and games like

☐ pin the tail on the donkey

☐ hopscotch

☐ racing

☐ _____ .

The **best** birthday present I ever received was

_____ .

My **dream** birthday present

would be _____

_____ .

Curious George loves to ride his **bike** and explore his neighborhood.

I learned to ride a bicycle with training wheels when I was _____ years old.

I learned to ride a bike without training wheels when I was _____ years old.

I ALSO like to ride (circle):

 puzzles

 gymnastics

 cook

play with my toys

 listen to music

help in the garden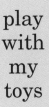

At home, these are the best things to do (circle):

dry dishes

 eat supper

read stories

daydream

Curious George is **always** eager to try new activities.
I'd be curious to try **these** for myself (circle):

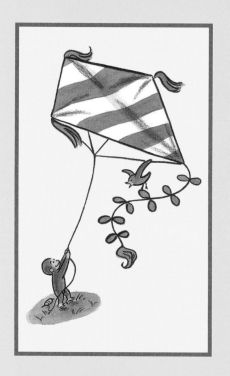

Curious About
My Day!

Since George is very curious, he loves to go to school to learn new things.

My **first** day of school was

_____ .

My school is named _____

_____ .

I am in

☐ preschool

☐ kindergarten

☐ _____ grade.

School starts at

_____ .

School ends at

_____ .

My teacher's name is

_____ .

I like my teacher because _____

_____

_____ .

My favorite subjects are (circle)...

art

math

PE

writing

reading

music

geography

science

I am **curious** to learn more about (circle)...

animals

making things

how things grow

how things work

space

nature

Curious George likes to **help** people.

I like to help **my teacher** by...

- ☐ listening during a lesson
- ☐ raising my hand before asking questions
- ☐ following classroom rules
- ☐ volunteering for special projects
- ☐ carrying supplies
- ☐ cleaning up
- ☐ staying in line

- ☐ _____

These are the names of other **people** who work in our **school:**

_____
teacher's aide

_____
janitor

_____
librarian

_____
gym teacher

_____
principal

A good way **our class** could help the **community** would be _____

_____

_____ .

Curious George loves to read!

I knew **all** my letters by the time **I was** _____ years old!

He reads at **school**, at **home**, and in the **library**. My favorite reading spot is

_____.

I learned to read when I was

_____ **years old.**

The **first book** I read by **myself** was _____

_____ .

Aa Bb Cc Dd Ee Ff Gg Hh Ii Jj Kk Ll Mm

This is a sample of my BEST handwriting:

Nn Oo Pp Qq Rr Ss Tt Uu Vv Ww Xx Yy Zz

Curious George loves to have a story read to him at bedtime.

☐ **I do, too!**
☐ **I read on my own.**

These are some of my favorite books:

(fill in the titles)

Here is a STORY I made up:

_____

_____

_____

_____

_____

_____

_____

_____

_____

_____

_____

The End

This is a picture of a character in one of my FAVORITE books:

Step 1

Start with George's eyes.

Step 2

Next comes George's face.

Step 3

Then draw George's nose.

Step 4

Give George a big smile!

You can draw Curious George!

You DID it!

Step 5

Add the top of George's head. Do you think George is starting to look like George?

Step 6

George's eyebrows and fur outline come next!

Step 7

Don't forget George's ear!

Field Trip

These are my favorite places to visit (circle):

aquarium

circus

museum

factory

firehouse

zoo

Curious About
Growing Up!

I am curious about these jobs.

Autographs

Autograph	Profession

I might like to do one of them when I grow up (circle):

Autograph	Profession

These are my predictions fo...

My future home will be

_____

_____

_____

_____

_____ .

Future Car (draw)

Future space travel

to _____

_____

the future.

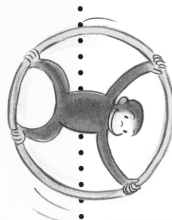

FUTURE ROBOT
(draw)

Future scientific discovery:

_____

_____

_____

_____

_____

!

FUTURE CLOTHES WE MIGHT WEAR

Here is **Curious George's** autograph:

George

· ·

And here is **mine!**

· ·

☑ **Curious George thinks you're great!**

☑ **There's no one else quite like you.**

☑ **Curious George would like to be your friend.**